Cinderella

mini GUPPY

For Audrey

FAIRYTALE FIASCO: CINDERELLA
is a GUPPY BOOK
Manufacturer: First published in Great Britain in 2026
by Guppy Publishing Ltd, Bracken Hill, Cotswold Road,
Oxford OX2 9JG

www.guppybooks.co.uk

Represented by: Authorised Rep Compliance Ltd, Ground Floor,
71 Lower Baggot Street, Dublin D02 P593, Ireland
www.arccompliance.com

ISBN: 9781916558502

1 3 5 7 9 10 8 6 4 2

Papers used by Guppy Books are from well-managed forests
and other responsible sources.

GUPPY PUBLISHING LTD Reg. No. 11565833
A CIP catalogue record for this book is available from
the British Library.

Typeset in Tarif Book by nesswood.co.uk
Printed and bound in China by Toppan Leefung

FSC
www.fsc.org
MIX
Paper | Supporting
responsible forestry
FSC® C104723

Fairytale Fiasco

Cinderella

Evgenia Golubeva
and Myles McLeod

mini GUPPY

Hello. I'm Cleo.

I'm seven and a half years old.

I like dressing up.

I like making up songs too.

And I LOVE making funny faces.

This is my room!

And this is my friend.

Mark LOVES reading.

He has read a million billion GAZILLION books.

CHAPTER ONE

It was time for a story.

Dad said, 'Right, Cleo! I'm going to make a cup of tea. Why don't you choose a book for me to read?'

I ran to my bookcase, closed my eyes and reached out my hand.

'I'd like a story that's fun,
with magic, a witch, or a whale.
So, one, two, three, I hope it will be
a fabulous fairytale.'

When poor Cinderella's mother died, her father soon married again.
Cinderella now had a cruel stepmother and two spoiled stepsisters. She was made to work in the kitchen from dawn till dusk.

Then the king invited everyone to a ball at the palace.
Cinderella wasn't allowed to go with her stepsisters.
No!
A fairy godmother cast a spell to help her.

At the ball, the prince fell in love with Cinderella.

And at midnight, she rushed away, leaving a glass slipper behind!

The prince searched high and low for someone who fitted the slipper perfectly.

At last Cinderella was discovered and she and the prince were married.

‘That’s a silly story!’ I said. ‘I’d tell that stepmum I’d never be her servant! I wouldn’t wait for a fairy godmother to save me. And all that kissing. UGH!’

'Would you like to help Cinderella?' asked Mark.

'Yes! Yes! Yes!' I said, bouncing on my bed.

'Good,' he said. 'But be careful. Don't turn it into a fairytale fiasco!'

ZIP and BOOM!
FLASH and KAZAM!

CHAPTER TWO

I found myself in a kitchen. I tried the door but it wouldn't open.

It's locked!

I turned around and saw a girl near the fireplace, sweeping up ashes.

'Hi! My name is Cleo! You must be Cinderella. I'm here to help you.'

‘Brilliant! I have to make dinner for everyone before they go to the ball!’ she said.

We walked to the cook's bench. There was flour and sugar and eggs and cream and butter and all sorts of things.

'Ooh!' I said. 'What are you making? I love mixing things.'

'Me too,' said Cinderella. 'I've been making bread. This time I thought it would be fun to mix in colours. Red from beetroot. Yellow from spices. Blue from berries.'

'I love it,' I said. 'Reminds me of my slime collection!'

'Slime?' said Cinderella, confused. 'Ugh. That doesn't sound very nice.'

'Not slug slime. Or frog slime. It's play-slime!' I explained.

I showed her how to mix cornstarch and soap together.

'See! Slime!' I said.

It sparkled, gold and pink. Wow!

We *squeezed* the slime.

Smushed the slime.

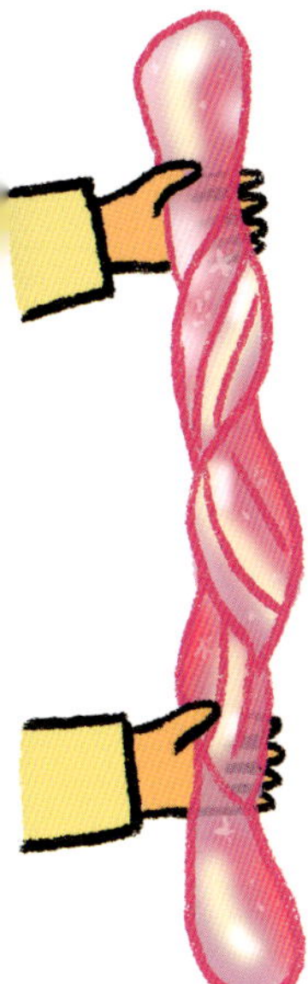

Twisted the slime.

Streeeeeetched the slime.

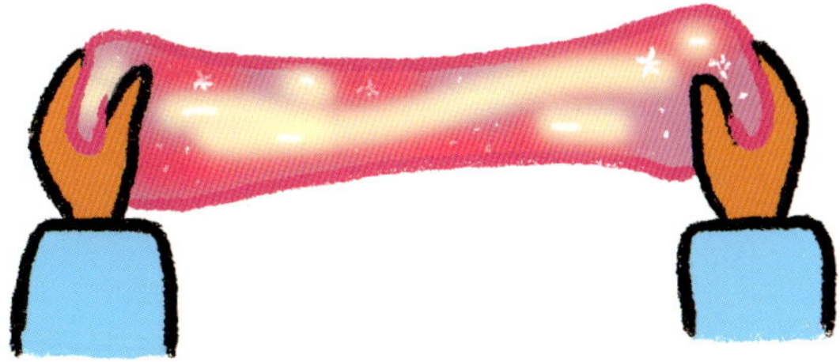

'I love it!' said Cinderella.

'So, when's the ball?' I asked.

'Tonight,' she said. 'I really want to go. But my stepmother Madame Lime said no.'

Just then, SNAP, the door was unlocked from the other side.

'Uh oh!' she said. 'That might be her now!'

But it wasn't!

CHAPTER THREE

It was Cinderella's stepsisters, Denise and Louise.

'I need you, Cinders! I can't choose which shoes to wear!' said Denise.

'You have to sort my hair too! I must look amazing for the prince,' cried Louise.

'And we are starving! Is dinner ready?' they asked.

They looked at the colourful, slimy mess on the table.

'Argh! Mama will be furious!' said Denise.

'What is it, anyway?' asked Louise.

I shared a purple, sparkly slime with them.

'Wow! So soft! And stretchy!' said Denise.

'And so relaxing!' said Louise.

We sat together, squeezing, smushing and twisting the slime. Denise and Louise didn't seem too bad. Just a bit spoiled.

‘Why does Cinderella do all the chores?’ I asked.

‘Dunno,’ said Denise. ‘Probably because she’s good at them.’

‘Plus I don’t want to do them,’ said Louise. ‘Bor-ring!’

'It might be fun if you all worked together,' I said.

'But Mama wouldn't allow it . . .' said Denise.

'Well, I'd tell your mum it's unfair!' I said.

'Stand up to Mama? No way!' said Denise, looking terrified.

But there was no need to look for her.

'What is all this mess? Where is the dinner? And who are you?' she demanded, pointing at me.

CHAPTER FOUR

Madame Lime pushed her daughters out of the room.

'Go and change into your best dresses! The carriage is waiting!' she shouted.

'And Cinderella! You've got work to do.'

'Oh please, Stepmother, let me go to the ball!' said Cinderella.

'Pah! Nobody would want to meet you with your dirty hair and your messy dress!' said Madame Lime.

It was so unfair. I had to say something. I gathered all my courage. 'Listen! I am Cleo! And I'm here to save Cinderella! She shouldn't be doing all the chores by herself,' I said.

'Of course! That's a perfectly good point,' she said to my surprise.

Now you're here, you can help her.

'Get to work! No time to waste,' she snapped and slammed the door shut, before locking it.

'Thank you for trying, Cleo!' said Cinderella. 'We'd better start on the to-do list.'

CHAPTER FIVE

I felt very sad for Cinderella and myself. The list of chores was endless.

But then I remembered something.

'Don't worry, Cinders! Help is on its way. Your fairy godmother's coming!' I said, filled with hope.

Suddenly the air
sparkled and glowed,
filling up with
the scent of roses.
WHOOSH!

‘Good afternoon, my dear Cinderella! Time to go to the ball!’ said the fairy godmother.

Then she noticed me.

'Oh, I didn't expect two of you. But don't worry, I've got enough magic for you both!' she said, and waved her wand.

Instantly my jeans and hoodie turned into a massive, frilly dress. Cinderella was given one too.

Both of us could hardly move and we looked like two giant puddings.

I grabbed a piece of charcoal and doodled some perfect dancing outfits.

The fairy godmother smiled and waved her wand again.

'That's more like it,' I said.

'Oooh! So comfortable!' said Cinderella as she practised some dance moves.

‘But what about the chores?’ she asked, looking around the messy kitchen.

I had another brilliant idea.

So, I drew a picture of one and the fairy godmother made it appear.

What a great idea, Cleo!

Then Cinderella looked at the clock. 'Oh no! The ball starts in five minutes. We'll never get there on time!'

CHAPTER SIX

The clock struck the hour. The ball was about to begin. The orchestra started playing but was interrupted by a loud noise from above. Everyone looked up and gasped.

Great idea, Cleo! I was going to suggest a carriage with horses, but this is much more fun!
That's amazing!
A flying machine!

I landed the helicopter in the castle garden. The king and queen rushed out to greet us.

'I love your outfit! So chic!' said the queen.

'Maybe I can have a go in your flying machine later?' suggested the king.

We made our way up the stairs and into the castle. There were so many guests . . . including Madame Lime, Denise and Louise. We froze on the spot. What if they saw us and made us go home?

But thanks to the fairy godmother's magic, they didn't recognise us at all! We headed for the dance floor.

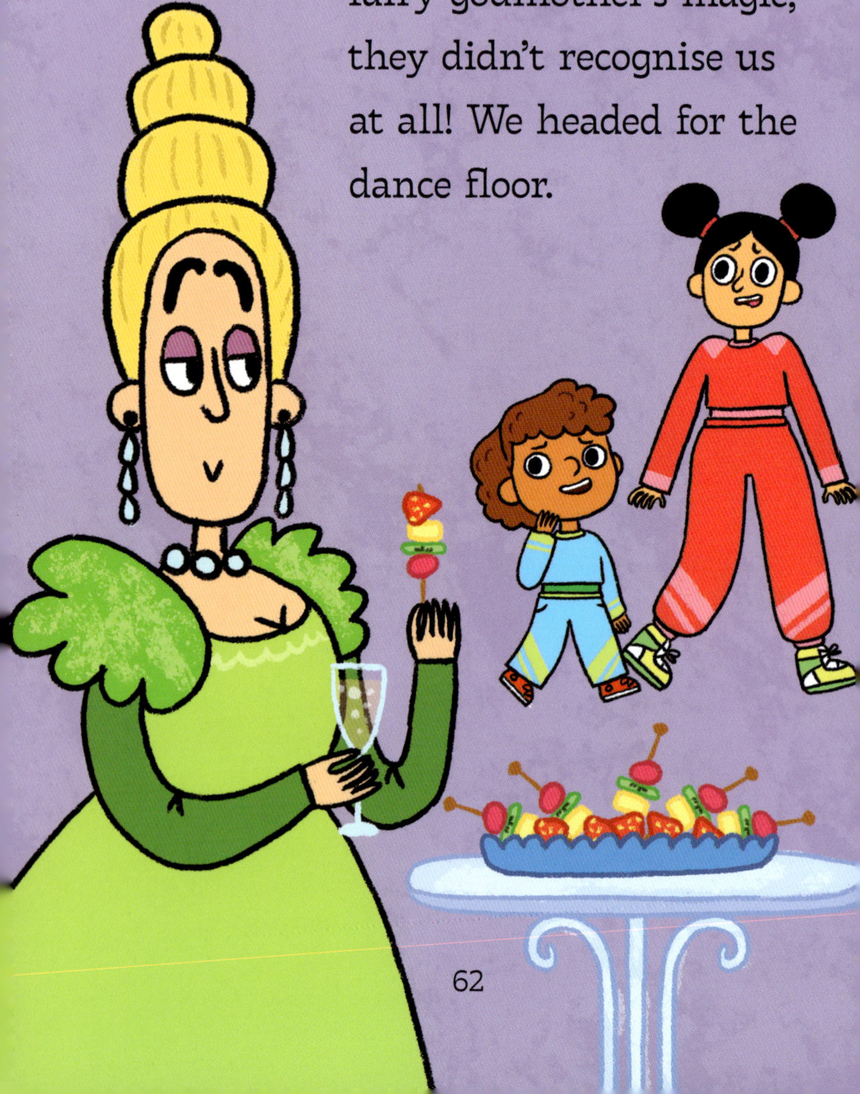

That's when I realised the orchestra was playing some old and very boring music.

'I can't dance to this!' I exclaimed.

'Much better!' I said, and we started dancing. Everyone else loved the new music too!

CHAPTER SEVEN

We danced and danced until we were dizzy. Cinderella and the prince both did some amazing moves.

I need a break!
Me too!

So we all flopped down on a squishy sofa.

'What else do you do at a ball?' I asked.

'Well, really it's just dancing and more dancing,' said the prince.

‘You should have a slime party,’ I said.

‘Slime?’ said the prince. ‘Ugh. That doesn’t sound very nice.’

‘You’ll like it,’ explained Cinderella. ‘It’s play-slime!’

Soon we had a table full of slime ingredients and we were making the biggest, best slimes ever. The other guests joined in too.

The prince and Cinderella seemed to be getting on really well.

Madame Lime was not happy about it.

'Those two strangers are ruining everything! I'm going to report them to the king for messing up the royal palace!'

She ran off to find the king and queen.

What a tell-tale!

I was so annoyed with her that I forgot to measure out the slime ingredients properly. When I mixed them together . . . oh no! They started to bubble and grow . . .

. . . and when Madame Lime returned with the king . . .

BO

. . . the slime exploded EVERYWHERE! What a fiasco!

'You'll be sent to the dungeons for this!' said Madame Lime with a nasty smile.

CHAPTER EIGHT

'Sorry, Dad,' said the prince to the king. The king looked down at himself and grinned. He grabbed a blob of slime and started squeezing and stretching and twisting it.

'Oh, I say, isn't this wonderful?' he said with glee. 'BEST PARTY EVER!'

Madame Lime looked like she'd sucked on a lemon.

Cinderella and I were having so much fun, but then the fairy godmother pointed at the clock. It was about to strike twelve!

'I forgot to say,' she said urgently. 'My magic runs out at midnight!'

'OH NO! If Madame Lime realises who we are, she'll be furious. RUN!'

We dashed out of the palace towards the helicopter.

As we went down the palace steps, Cinderella's sneaker plopped into a load of slime and came off.

'Just like the glass slipper,' I said to myself.

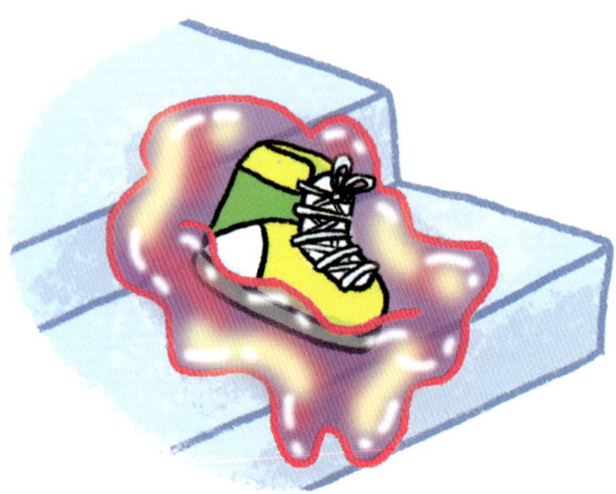

CHAPTER NINE

As the clock struck for the twelfth time, the fairy godmother disappeared and her magic came to an end!

We rushed home, holding hands and laughing. We'd had such a good time.

We ran to the kitchen and pretended nothing had happened. The robot cleaner had been really busy and done an amazing job of tidying.

Wow!

Nice work, Robert!
Thank you!
You are welcome!

A moment later, the door opened. It was Denise and Louise.

They told us all about the ball. They didn't know we had been there the whole time!

'And best of all,' said Denise, 'the prince found a shoe on the stairs, stuck in some slime. It belonged to one of the mystery guests. He's visiting every house tomorrow. He's looking for the one who fits the shoe!'

'It's a size six,' said Louise. 'I'm almost a size six, so maybe he'll think it was me.'

'I'd like to try that shoe,' said Cinderella with a wink.

The door opened again. It was Madame Lime.

'Denise! Louise! Time for bed!'

They rushed out and she turned to us.

'And time for you two to begin preparing breakfast,' said Madame Lime. 'And don't think you'll be seeing the prince when he comes! No way!'

She snapped the door closed again. CLICK. Locked!

CHAPTER TEN

The next day, the prince came to visit.

'I'm looking everywhere for the owner of this slimy shoe! She's awesome,' said the prince.

'My daughters will try the shoe!' said Madame Lime.

Oh, if only he knew it belonged to me, he'd rescue me.

But then Cinderella shook her head and said, 'What am I saying, Cleo? I'm going to save myself!'

She grabbed the robot cleaner and took it to the locked door.

'Come on, Robert,' she said. 'Clean this door! Maximum clean!'

The robot cleaner started cleaning. It cleaned and polished the door. It cleaned and polished, cleaned and polished, and cleaned and polished some more. It didn't stop.

'That's it,' said Cinderella, 'keep going!'

Soon the robot had cleaned a hole right through the door.

CHAPTER ELEVEN

Denise tried on the slimy shoe.

'It fits!' she cried.

Louise tried on the slimy shoe.

'It fits me too!' she said with glee.

Even Madame Lime
tried the shoe on.

'And it fits me! Oh my!'

The prince nodded sadly.

'That's the problem. It's a size six. It fits loads of people. It could belong to anyone!'

'No, it couldn't,' I said as Cinderella and I burst into the room.

'That's right,' said Cinderella. 'It's mine and I'll prove it!' She looked inside the sneaker.

'See!' she said. 'I put name tags in my shoes. I didn't want to lose them!'

‘I found you!’ said the prince happily.

‘Oh wow, Cinders,’ said Denise. ‘It was you at the ball. Does this mean you’re getting married to the prince?’

‘Married?!’ said the prince, surprised.

‘Don’t be silly,’ I said. ‘They only met last night!’

‘Actually, I was hoping we could talk about slime,’ said Cinderella.

‘Oh yeah!’ said the prince.

Enough!
I'm going to lock you all in the kitchen! Even the prince!

Oh no you're not!

CHAPTER TWELVE

After that . . . everyone lived happily ever after. Sort of! Madame Lime was ordered to clean the palace from top to bottom. It was time for *her* to do some tidying!

Cinderella and the prince did still fall in love. Ugh! But they also set up an amazing slime business. Denise and Louise helped too. And the robot cleaner was useful for mixing and cleaning up slimy spills.

And the fairy godmother came back just to give the king a ride in her helicopter.

Then I saw someone familiar in the castle gardens.

Mark. Book Mark!

'Ready to go home, Cleo?' he asked.

'Ready,' I said.

Farewell, fairytale!

CHAPTER THIRTEEN

I found myself back in my bed, with a pot of sparkling Cinderella Slime.

Dad arrived with his cup of tea.

'Where did that goo come from?' he said. 'You'll have to wash your hands again.'

He took a blob.

'Fun!' he said.

Then (after we'd washed our hands) he opened the book and started to read.

'Once upon a time, there was a girl called Cinderella . . .

‘She was busy working in the kitchen, when another girl called Cleo appeared.’

Dad stopped, surprised.

‘This isn’t the story I remember!’ he said.

THE END

Fairytale FIASCO

If you loved this book,
look out for:

Coming soon:
SLEEPING BEAUTY and
JACK AND THE BEANSTALK